For Olivia with all my love AM

For my Parents MC

Published by Delacorte Press
Bantam Doubleday Dell Publishing Group, Inc.
666 Fifth Avenue, New York, New York 10103

This edition was originally published
in Great Britain in 1990 by ABC
First American edition published in September 1991

Text copyright © 1990 by Angela McAllister
Illustrations copyright © 1990 by Margaret Chamberlain

Library of Congress Cataloging in Publication Data applied for

ISBN 0-385-30326-2   0-385-30327-0 (lib bdg)
Printed and bound in Hong Kong by Imago Services (H.K.) Ltd

10 9 8 7 6 5 4 3 2 1

The Enchanted Flute *

Written by Angela McAllister * Illustrated by Margaret Chamberlain

Delacorte
Press

Queen Pernickety was AWFULLY fussy.

She was never happy with a plum, a tiara, or a new toothbrush until she was absolutely sure that nobody else had one quite as nice. Her needlewomen sewed all night to make frocks and bloomers with more sequins than anyone had ever seen before. But if the Queen noticed bloomers more sparkly than hers on somebody else's washing line she would stamp her feet and send all the needlewomen to the dungeon to thread one hundred needles.

Every day her chef had to create a new dish that was more lip-smackingly scrumptious than anyone had ever tasted before. But if the Queen remembered eating a pudding just as delicious at somebody else's house she would stamp her feet and order the chef to peel enough onions to make him cry ten bucketfuls of tears.

Everybody worked from cock crow to candle stump, to please
fussy Queen Pernickety. And although her weary subjects tried
hard to love her, they all found it grumblingly difficult.

The only person who truly loved the fussy Queen was her daughter, Princess Olivia. Luckily nobody else had a daughter quite as nice. She was good as gold, merry as a cricket, bright as a button, fair as a lily, and was loved by everybody in the Queendom.

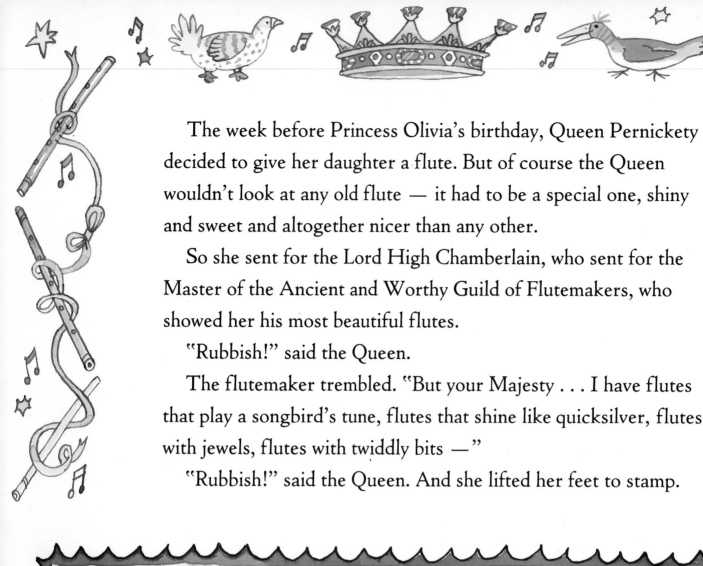

The week before Princess Olivia's birthday, Queen Pernickety decided to give her daughter a flute. But of course the Queen wouldn't look at any old flute — it had to be a special one, shiny and sweet and altogether nicer than any other.

So she sent for the Lord High Chamberlain, who sent for the Master of the Ancient and Worthy Guild of Flutemakers, who showed her his most beautiful flutes.

"Rubbish!" said the Queen.

The flutemaker trembled. "But your Majesty . . . I have flutes that play a songbird's tune, flutes that shine like quicksilver, flutes with jewels, flutes with twiddly bits —"

"Rubbish!" said the Queen. And she lifted her feet to stamp.

The desperate flutemaker had an idea. "There is an old goldsmith . . . I am sure he could make something extraordinary."

So the Queen sent for the goldsmith.

A bent old man arrived with a white beard so long that it was still trailing through the door when he himself had reached the throne.

Mumbling gruff apologies, he stuffed his beard into the many pockets of his cloak. Then he bowed so low he poked himself in the eye with a toe sticking out of a hole in his shoe.

Queen Pernickety was not impressed. But the goldsmith was her last hope. She commanded him to make her the most extraordinary flute, more special than any other, gave him a new pair of shoes, and told him to come back the following day.

The next afternoon, the old goldsmith returned and presented Queen Pernickety with a small flute.

When the Queen saw it she was outraged.

"It doesn't shine, it isn't even silver, it hasn't got any jewels, it hasn't got one twiddly bit . . . it's RUBBISH!"

And she raised the royal feet for an almighty stamp.

But the goldsmith bent closer. "Things, your Majesty, may not always be what they seem . . ." he whispered mysteriously. "Whoever listens to the music of this flute will hear the sound most dear to his heart, whatever it may be."

The Queen was right royally amazed. "Is this the only one?"

The goldsmith nodded. "It is the first flute I have ever made."

The Queen was delighted and paid the goldsmith twice his weight in groceries and a few more shoes in her excitement.

When Princess Olivia unwrapped the flute on her birthday she squeaked with thrills. She started to play and heard the sound most dear to her heart . . . the sweetest flute music that ever charmed a breeze.

But Queen Pernickety heard something quite different . . .

From the goldsmith's flute came the praising voices of all her subjects — "You have the prettiest parasol, your Highness . . . oh, the handsomest horses, your Majesty . . . just the most stunning slippers, your royal Wonderfulness . . ."

"Don't stop, don't stop!" cried the Queen in a swoon.

But Princess Olivia was already dancing out the door, playing as she went. She skipped past the Lord High Chamberlain, who heard, to his astonishment, the lullaby his mother used to sing. And before you could say "bedtime for bunnikins," his thumb was in his mouth.

On the princess played, into the town, where everyone heard the sound most dear to his heart — some heard the gulls and the tide-wind song of the sea; some heard the melody of a maypole dance; the children heard nursery rhymes and cuckoos. Everyone was happy when the princess passed.

When the goldsmith saw how all the tired people were cheered by the sound of the flute, he bolted his door, pulled down the shutters, and set about making more flutes.

For three days and nights, the goldsmith's shop rumbled with strange chants. Puffs of colored smoke and starry sparkles shot out of his chimney and not a curious cat would creep close.

When the shutters were opened at last, there were a dozen new flutes for sale in the window.

But before one flute could be sold, Queen Pernickety heard what the goldsmith had done. She stamped her feet and shouted at the Lord High Chamberlain. "How can Princess Olivia have the very best flute if there are A DOZEN MORE JUST THE SAME!"

"Yes . . . no . . . I mean never . . . not if I can help it . . . straightaway your Highness," stuttered the Lord High Chamberlain. And he sent a dozen guards to destroy the new flutes and then hid in the garden shed while Queen Pernickety rampaged in a stamping storm through the palace.

Nobody knew that the goldsmith was really a good-hearted magician who had only wanted to make the people happy.

And the guards didn't know they had been sent to destroy a dozen *enchanted* flutes . . .

They tried to bend and break them, they dropped them from the highest tower, they flung them into a fiery furnace — but enchanted flutes cannot be destroyed. Finally, in despair, they tied a sack of cabbages to each one and tossed them into a deep, muddy river.

But Queen Pernickety was AWFULLY fussy. When she heard the flutes had not been destroyed she stopped the Lord High Chamberlain's puddings for a week. Then she confiscated all the goldsmith's shoes and banished him from the Queendom.

That evening, as the barefoot old goldsmith left the realm of Queen Pernickety, he cast one last spell.

The next day, when Princess Olivia played her flute, everyone ran away in horror — for now they were hearing the sounds their hearts most feared. Some heard sea shanties of shipwrecks, some heard thunder grumbles, and the children heard the snap of crocodiles' jaws. Everyone was upset when the princess passed.

But the princess, who had no fears in her heart, heard only the toots and trills of flute music. She could not understand why the people fled.

When she skipped past the garden shed, the Lord High Chamberlain was awakened by the flute. It sounded to him like the Queen's feet stamping, so loud that he put a flowerpot on his head.

Then into the throne room Princess Olivia played her flute. And what Queen Pernickety heard made her go white as a pillowcase — the voices of her tired, groaning subjects telling her THE TRUTH!

"You overwork us, always demanding better than best, Queen Fusspot . . . the people do not love you just because you have the finest things, your proud Majesty . . . you have the fanciest frocks but the hardest heart, your selfish Sovereignness."

Queen Pernickety felt so ashamed that she blushed a royal ruby red, and the most sparkling teardrop in the Queendom trickled down her cheek.

Princess Olivia stopped playing and hugged her mother tight.

"Do you love me, Olivia?" asked the Queen, hopefully.

"Of course, Mother, with all my heart." The princess laughed.

"Then all is not yet lost. I have been such a silly, foolish fusspot, always demanding the better than best of everything. I have not stopped to think of my overworked, exhausted subjects, only of myself. I've been a downright, dreadful disgrace." The Queen dried her eyes with the daintiest of handkerchiefs. "But today we shall announce a month's holiday throughout the Queendom and start with a Grand Carnival Party. Nobody shall work — you and I will hang the decorations together and I shall make all the sandwiches. They might not be the very best sandwiches, but that won't matter as long as everybody has a jolly good time."

"Then I shall play my flute!" said the princess. And before the Queen had time to cover her ears, she heard . . . the sweetest flute music that ever charmed a breeze!

And that was all that anybody ever heard from the enchanted flute. The Queen had learned her lesson. She became so easy to please that the people had much less work to do and could all go fishing every Wednesday.

The goldsmith magician never returned to the realm of Queen Pernickety. But his twelve enchanted flutes still lie somewhere at the bottom of a deep, muddy river.